When Millypop and Her Mummy Visited Ice Cream Land...

Reka Hall

When Millypop and Her Mummy Visited Ice Cream Land...

Olympia Publishers
London

www.olympiapublishers.com
OLYMPIA PAPERBACK EDITION

A CIP catalogue record for this title is available from the British Library.

ISBN: 978-1-78830-703-1

First Published in 2020

Olympia Publishers
Tallis House
2 Tallis Street
London
EC4Y 0AB

Printed in Great Britain

Dedication

To Emily,

My lovely daughter,
I wrote this book to keep your dreams safe during the night. When you told me about Ice Cream Land, I knew that there were many children out there who couldn't sleep during the night because it's dark and can be scary. I wanted to share your story with the world and see if your inspiration could help others. Your ideas and imagination are truly amazing, and I hope you will never stop dreaming about this magical space among many others as I love hearing your new adventures every morning about your safe place.

I am looking forward to reading our story with you with a hot chocolate and wonder around in Ice Cream Land. I hope you will never stop the way you see the world as you are truly an inspiration. Love you,

Mum

Millypop almost turned 5. She came home from school one day and everything was how it should be. She had her dinner then had her shower - she loved the shower because her mummy let her blow bubbles in the bathroom. She then brushed her teeth. Soon after she read a story to her mummy. She was particularly proud of reading the story herself.

Her mummy was about to say 'Night night, love you, see you in the morning,' when she said to her mummy with teary eyes,

"I can't sleep Mummy – I am scared."

"What happened?" asked her mummy.

"I had a bad dream yesterday," explained Millypop.

Her mummy thought 'That's not like you,' but Millypop's mummy had an idea and she said

"It's ok Millypop, let's play a game, that will keep your mind off this bad dream."

Millypop agreed sobbing. Her mummy asked what was Millypop's favourite place in the whole wide world.

"Ice Cream Land," she said.

"Great," said her mummy, "And what does Ice Cream Land look like?" asked her mummy.

"There is ice cream everywhere Mummy, like the trees outside," said Millypop.

"That is brilliant," said her mummy. "And what colour are they?" asked her mummy.

"They are pink, purple, red, yellow… all the rainbow colours," said Millypop.

"And what else?" asked her mummy.

Millypop thought hard and with a smile on her face started telling her mummy what Ice Cream Land looked like.

"There is a marshmallow bouncy castle Mummy, come and jump with me," she said, and they did.

"There are slides Mummy made of chocolate, a bumpy one, and a big one. Come and try them out with me," she said, and they did.

"There is a see-saw and it's made of Smarties. Come with me Mummy, let's try it out," she said, and they tried it out.

As they went on a path made of different shaped cupcakes they saw an enormous unicorn cake. It had 4 tiers covered with vanilla icing (it looked like a mountain). It had a huge rainbow horn on the top. While they were thinking how they could climb it, they noticed a tunnel through it. Inside it was rainbow coloured and tasted like a chocolate cake with raspberry jam and sprinkles.

As they passed the huge cake mountain and explored more of Ice Cream Land, they saw chocolate rabbits hopping away. They saw giant jelly mushrooms wobbling away.

"Come on Mummy hop with me on the giant jellies like the chocolate rabbits," said Millypop, so they hopped from one mushroom to another…

Until they reached an enormous chocolate waterfall and a chocolate lake under it. It was made of white, dark and milk chocolate with a big overarching rainbow. There was a pot of golden chocolate coins next to it with a note.

"Look Mummy, there is a pot of golden coins – chocolate coins," Millypop shouted.

She read the note, "T-O MIL-LY-POP: THR-O-W A CO-I-N IN-TO THE CHO-CO-LA-TE LA-KE AND MA-KE A WISH."

Millypop picked up one of the golden coins and threw it in the chocolate lake in front of the waterfall and thought very hard what to wish for.

"I wish, we could come to Ice Cream Land every evening Mummy, so I wouldn't have any more bad dreams," said Millypop.

Her mummy gave her the biggest cuddle with teary eyes and could only say, "I love you Millypop."

After all this adventure, they were a bit hungry. Millypop asked her mummy to help getting some of the ice cream. Her mummy helped Millypop and got some too of the yummy ice cream from the rainbow coloured ice cream trees. They were everywhere popping up, one after the other, in Ice Cream Land.

Millypop and her mummy thought it was time to head back, so they hopped back on the wobbly giant jelly mushrooms. They went through the tunnel of the huge unicorn cake mountain and tasted the rainbow coloured chocolate cake with raspberry jam and sprinkles again, as it was delicious. Played on the Smarties see-saw. Played on the chocolate slides. The bumpy one and the big one. Bounced on the marshmallow bouncy castle and felt happy, as they knew they could come back the next evening and the one after that, and the one after that.

Next to the marshmallow bouncy castle there was a grass field. The grass was made of gummy bears. Millypop felt a bit tired after all that fun and had an idea.

"Come on Mummy, let's lie on the gummy bear grass and look at the clouds, they are made of candy floss," she said, and they lied down counting the candy floss clouds. 1,2,3,4,5…

Millypop finally fell asleep on the gummy bear grass peacefully and continued thinking of her favourite place in the whole wide world.

Her mummy kissed goodnight to Millypop. "Sleep tight my Millypop."

And Millypop dreamt all night about Ice Cream Land and the adventures they had.